LOOK WHO'S TALKING

LOOK WHO'S TALKING

Harnisha Singh

Vij Books India Pvt Ltd

New Delhi (India)

Published by

Vij Books India Pvt Ltd
(Publishers, Distributors & Importers)
2/19, Ansari Road
Delhi – 110 002
Phones: 91-11-43596460, 91-11-47340674
Mobile: 98110 94883
e-mail: contact@vijpublishing.com
www.vijbooks.in

ISBN: 978-93-90439-27-0 (Paperback)
ISBN: 978-93-90439-35-5 (ebook)

This book is dedicated to my parents,

Major General Harish Jit Singh, SC, VSM
and
Mrs. Nishi Singh.

When others compliment me,

Or look at me with admiration,

I thank those two pair of hands,

That shaped me, sculpted me,

And nurtured my vision.

Love, gratitude, sabr, shukr,

They laid down the best foundation,

My parents, my life force,

I owe it all to them,

They are my motivation,

They are my inspiration.

CONTENTS

ACKNOWLEDGEMENTS

As my debut novel goes into print, it all feels a bit surreal. 'Gratitude is the most exquisite form of courtesy' - Jacques Maritain, and I have a long list of people I would like show my gratitude to.

Thank you Mom and Dad, for giving me that first vote of confidence. It is your immense belief in me that has motivated me to write this book. Thank you Mandeep, for being the most amazing partner anyone could ever have, you are the wind beneath my wings and I Love you!

Thank you Bhai – Gunraj Singh, for introducing me to the world of books and encouraging me to read since childhood. Our lifelong banter has helped me develop a sense of humor.

Thank you mom and dad (my second set of parents), my in laws, for your blessing and best wishes.

Thank you Navreet, Japna, Prabhjot Arora Bro, Shivi, Sidhi, Deepak, Shafali and Kavita, for encouraging me to write, being my sounding board and giving me valuable feedback.

Thank you Vij Publications, for believing in this book and making me an author. So grateful!

And above all, thank you Waheguruji, without your blessings, none of this would have been possible.

Chapter 1

LOOK WHO'S TALKING

Last night was dreadfully catastrophic. A disturbingly disastrous debacle. Absolutely precarious. Totally unwarranted and needless. Highly hazardous. An entirety of unnecessary hooliganism.

You get the gist of my emotion, right? Dramatic much? Not at all!! You see, I distinctly ordered normalcy and serenity, with extra peace on the side, but was served a concoction of fear and anxiety, infused with generous toppings of confusion and chaos instead. I had to succumb to this unpalatable entrée. So yes, I'm cross, and whosoever is in charge around here, I'd like to have a word with that person.

You may accuse me of being a tad bit belligerent, but can you blame me? I barely got any sleep last night due to the aforementioned servings on my platter. Much to my dismay, I'm feeling the heat of it this morning, so kindly pardon my bed head, my rant, and my sleep deprived chronicles. I promise to do better once I catch up on my sleep. For now, I am going to be unnecessarily flippant, and tirade to my heart's content about last night's avoidable euphoric shenanigans.

Yes, I understand it's New Year's Eve, but people, why be so loud? And why burst crackers? All that ruckus and commotion has been of such grave inconvenience to those like me who love a good night's sleep. Thanks to all you noisy *party animals*, I am grouchy and cranky today. And me, not being on my best behavior, is on you! *Venting is good. I'm feeling better already.* ☺

Oh, I'm sorry, you must think I'm rude to have not introduced myself yet. My name is Mithi and I'm not sure about my actual age, but people say I look young and beautiful. They are right! By the way, Happy New Year to you all. New Year brings new hope and new aspirations. I don't desire much, all I wish is that this year treats me better and kinder, as opposed to previous years.

Hey look! I see visitors at the gate. It's the beginning of a new year, so we are expecting some nice people over. They usually come bearing gifts. Love it! Happy times ahead. Let's see what this lady and gentleman have brought for us. I have not met these two before, as I'm new here, but they are familiar with others around.

I think I should go greet them and bedazzle them with my personality and happy dance, which is already a super hit here amongst all. And if you'll insist, I shall happily share the happy dance steps for you to follow. I'm bit of a self-taught expert on it, and I can assure you that it's easy and is sure to win hearts. Do put on your dancing shoes, because this dance involves a fine, synchronized combination of movements. Let me sing it to you – repeat after me.

Wag your tail,

Wiggle your butt,

Sway your head &

Jiggle your gut.

Yes, tail... Why?

Did I not mention before? Oh, my apologies. I'm a doggo and I have a tail. Statutory warning, if you are human, do not do the happy dance. It is only for Doggos.

Alright, the visitors are approaching, I see them, and they are in possession of a bag containing lot of treats. Aha! I love treats. Will try to confiscate the bag. Wish me luck! See you in a bit with more updates!

Time to put my best paw forward,

Activate happy dance,

And make them fall in love with me,

At first glance.

Chapter 2

EVERY DOG HAS HIS DAY

New Year, new day, new beginnings ~

Like a blank canvas.

Paint it right,

Earthy hues or bright, dark or light,

Be the artist of your life.

What a beautiful day, indeed. Sitting in my balcony, with my morning cup of coffee, I admire the sieved rays of sunlight falling on my plants, nourishing them, giving them life. Basking in the yellow light, my plants are growing newer leaves, lush and green, day by day. Metamorphosis of any kind - in life, in nature, in objects, is so inspiring. Lost in my comatose thoughts, I lose track of time.

'Nishaaa…', I hear Mandeep, my husband, calling out to me from inside the house. Waking up from my meditative stupor, I go to our bedroom and give him my customary good morning kiss along with a complimentary New Year kiss. I smile thinking about our marriage and relationship having endured metamorphosis too in the last decade.

Breakfast time beckons; toast, eggs and juice is ready on the table. Wasting no time lazing around after breakfast, we promptly get dressed and load our car. All set, we get going. We have special plans for the day. With the intention to start the year with good karma and a clean slate, my husband and I, decided to visit the Animal shelter and rehabilitation farm with a carload of dog treats and ration for the rescued inmates there.

Yes, rehabilitation is not just a fancy term for celebrities in addiction recovery; it's also for all the unfortunate, abused, injured and abandoned animals as well.

Having great admiration for the work the rehabilitation shelter does for the voiceless, I, as a volunteer, would often visit them to help and support in whatever way deemed possible and necessary.

The farm provides food and shelter to an assortment of animals, majorly dogs. You can find a myriad of four legged (sometimes three or two, one or none, due to amputation and mangle), abandoned, bewildered, damaged, yet hopeful dogs, looking for a safe haven to call it home.

So here we are, at this happy place, where anyone who would want to donate, foster, adopt, volunteer, help or just spend some quality time with the animals, is most welcome.

Being greeted and cheered by these multitudes of pedigreed and non-pedigreed fur balls, all different in size, shape, color and temperament, has always been therapeutic for me. The urgent noses, impatient paws, eager tails, earnest tongues - I love everything about this place, except maybe, the acoustics. The noise decibels are understandably appalling, wherein if one dog barks, the rest join in, in a fever pitch, of un-synced symphony. Word of caution, it's not the place to visit with a hangover, after a long night of celebration. Point noted for future reference ;-)

Entering the farm, we are as usual greeted first by the 'over enthusiastic', the 'forever brimming with boundless energy' kind of dogs, jumping around excitedly, and just being the happy dogs that they all deserve to be. They demand pampering, lots of pets, head rubs, belly rubs, and of course, treats. We indulge them all, every dog has its way. Playing with them and petting them, we walk towards Nik, the caretaker, at the oasis of the farm. I see some new furry faces around, some look happy and some are skeptical, warily approaching us. They all get treats. A few are tied to a leash owing to their unpredictable temperaments, rest are all let loose, being constantly monitored by their caretakers.

Amongst others, I am approached by this little black puppy, wiggling and wagging her little backside and her scrawny little tail so vigorously, that even her belly and her face move and sway side by side. 'Looks like the little one is dancing', I say to Mandeep, laughingly.

The puppy seems to be about 5-6 months old, cross breed between a mongrel and a Labrador, has tiny twisted ears, and a very small face. She gobbles up the treats I give her, looks mighty pleased, and then starts to bounce on all fours, asking for more I reckon. She does get some more treats and some more petting, before my attention is diverted to other dogs, waiting for their turn. The whole 'meet and greet, pet and rub, show some love, share some treats' routine takes time, and all this while, I notice the little black puppy, following me, shadowing me.

Chapter 3

GONE TO THE DOGS

Hi again! This is Mithi reporting live from the farms of rescueville. Happy to announce, I ate a lot of treats, could have eaten much more, but the stingy lady, (she is called Nisha), won't give me the 'doggie bag'. Tried many high jumps, but could not reach the said bag. All treats are gone to the dogs now (literally).

I got ample pets and hugs too. These two humans are quite nice and generous with love, not so generous with treats though. Now I'm happily tailing them around. This feels natural. Like an invisible leash is pulling me towards them. They are pampering me. I am feeling safe in their company. Am a happy doggo.

Wish more people were kind to us dogs. What possible pleasures could be attained by some people from hitting us with sticks, stones or bare hands? Why do some people feel no remorse injuring us, abandoning us on the roads or running us over with their vehicles? Don't people realize that we feel pain just as much, that we are sentient too?

I would not bore you with the details of my traumatic past predicament, and how I was abused and then left alone and abandoned on the road. But let me tell you, that me, and many other dogs like me, are distraught and distressed beyond belief. Yes, juxtaposition to our happy demeanor.

For the records, we dogs would never abandon our humans, come what may. No matter what course their life might take, we dogs always remain faithful and are always by their side.

Two months back, I was rescued from these scary roads. Thankfully, some kind hearted humans spotted me and took pity on me, while I was scavenging for food. I admit I looked hideous. Sickness and starvation had taken a toll on me and my appearance. I was in pain from several injuries and I was hungry. I had numerous itchy bald patches on me, of which I am embarrassed to talk about. Also, I had a nasty cough.

I was apparently taken to a veterinary, who inserted a strange object into my unmentionable body part, pierced needles in my body, made me ingest pills, and to compensate for all the grave travesties he performed on me, gave me loads of treats to eat. So I forgave him.

The state I was in, depicted the descent of my well-being, hence I was then brought to my current location, away from the dangers of roads and vehicles, where in, I am getting better now. I made a few human and dog friends here, they gave me a name too, 'Mithi', meaning sweet, because I am a sweetheart. I also have my own food and water bowl along with a woolen coat that I am made to wear at night because of the chilly winter cold nights. Life is good now. My past sufferings and my traumatic ordeal, quite like Voldemort's name, is something I don't speak of. But when I sleep, I have nightmares.

Returning back from my flashback, bringing to you my current update, I am still following the lady around, getting more than my fair share of attention and love. Yes I'm a shameless hogger, and you may judge me all you want. Go ahead, judge me, see if I care, but the lady is finally giving all her attention to me, talking to me, in soft, gentle tones, and I'm elated. My caretaker friend and these visitors are simultaneously talking about something, serious I guess, and I hear my name time and again, in their conversation. I don't bother to eavesdrop; I am in doggo heaven, this lady is doing a great job giving me the best belly rubs.

The touch of her hands on my body is so soothing. I have waited so long to be stroked with such kindness and love. *More, more!!! A little bit here, a little bit there too!!! Yes that's the spot!!* Let me twist and angle my body for maximum massage coverage. I am flexible that ways.

Wait, what? Why did you stop?? *Don't stop lady. And where do you think you are going?* She gave me a huge kiss on my snout, mumbled something to me, and got up to leave with her husband. I don't understand. *We were having fun, weren't we?* I cannot fathom anything more important than the heavy petting (no obvious crude double entendre pun intended) we were into.

Get back now and love me lady! I was just beginning to fall in love with you.

Chapter 4

THE DWARF WHO STOLE MY HEART

Life is an ambiguity of surreal tragedy,

Be resilient and face your reality.

Speaking with Nik, and simultaneously playing with the dogs around us, Mandeep and I are not able to take our eyes off the little black dancing puppy called 'Mithi'. There is something about her that is making her stand out. Maybe it is her inbred imperfections, her jubilance or the way she is looking at us. We wanted to know more about her, her rescue and her healing wounds. Mithi had been following us ever since, and regaling us with her lovable antics.

We are surprised to learn that this pup, is actually, not really a pup, but a full grown, approximately five or six years old, dwarf dog. Her stunted growth and unconventional looks could have made her an easy target of abandonment by her previous owner, or probably she was a breeder's reject due to her dwarfism and mixed lineage.

When Mithi was rescued, she was apparently in a terribly sad condition, suffering from mange, kennel cough and open wounds. A bag of bones, she was found famished and fatigued. Because of her trauma, Mithi suffers from anxiety and nightmares at night. She cries and shivers in her sleep. My heart breaks hearing this.

In spite of her small size, her resilience to fight all odds, stay alive, protect herself from her adversaries, is awe inspiring and it deeply touches my heart.

The rescue saga of Mithi, the impediments and ordeal of this little dog, fill my heart and eyes. I cannot stop my tears, and cannot hold myself back from giving her all the love I can muster.

She, in turn, is blissfully delighted and receptive of all my love and attention. I see her not letting me out of her sight. There is an underlying connection between us; one we did not know existed. Mandeep feels it too. He sees the instant bond and that special connect between us. It was effortless. Karmic connection, he says. So, when I look at him beseechingly, his words echo my thoughts.

'Let's adopt her', Mandeep says, smiling at me.

I would have hugged him if I were not covered in dog hair and drool. My happiness knows no bounds and I am over the moon. It feels so right, we do not have to think twice about it. Even though, we came here today with no such intention, everything seems to be falling into place. Nik too, is very supportive of our decision, and asks us to complete the paperwork as soon as possible, have our home check review done by another volunteer, and thereafter, take Mithi home.

I decide I don't want to wait. I cannot wait. I will not have Mithi spend another night in the cold, fighting her nightmares alone. Requesting the designated volunteer to conduct the home visit as soon as possible today itself, I tell Nik we would come back after the formalities are done and over with, to take Mithi home later in the evening.

I give Mithi a kiss on her snout, and promise her I'll be back for her. This little black dog, who stole my heart, looks at me with big, brown, pleading eyes, asking me to stay a little while longer.

I need to leave, I can't stay longer even though I want to. The sooner the paperwork and formalities are commenced, the sooner they'll end and we'll be able to take Mithi home hence.

I want today, to be the first day of the rest of her new life.

Chapter 5

I HAVE BEEN DOGNAPPED

Trivia: Can dogs feel a hangover?

Answer: Yes, we can (Speaking from experience).

I'm a doggo and I think I know now, what a happy hangover feels like. I am still revelling in the awesomeness of today's morning events. I can still sniff the lady's aroma on my fur and can still feel her soft lips on my snout. Even though I was left asking for more, I am grateful for this day bestowed upon me. It almost makes up for last night's debauchery, though I worked my charms like a player through my sleep deprived anonymity like a pro. At the risk of repeating myself, I am a happy doggo. It's been a lovely day today and I am going to sleep mighty peacefully tonight, come what may. Sweet dreams my friends, see you all tomorrow.

(At sleep time)

Uhh, what's going on? What is all this commotion at the gate?

We have visitors?

Again?

At this time?

My sleep time? Nooooooo….

Aaahaaa! Look who's back! Could not resist my charm, could you!!

Hi lady, welcome back. Yes I missed you too. You got more treats? Give me pets. More!! more!!

Wooah! Why am I being taken on a leash? Should I be alarmed? I feel like a prisoner in chains, being taken to the dreaded gallows. Did I do something wrong? Am I being evicted? The lady is now holding my leash, and taking me out. OMG, I think I am being dognapped? HELP! I REPEAT, SEND IMMIDIATE HELP!!

Why are the caretakers saying goodbye to me? Save me guys, don't smile at my kidnappers. Can you believe it; my caretakers are hand in glove in this fiasco of my dognapping. I will not make it easy for them. I will fight. I will bite. My bite will be worse than my bark. I will…. Ohh, they picked me up and put me in the backseat of their car. How dare they! I forgot to bite. Now they are asking me if I'm comfortable. I will not respond. I choose to ignore them.

The lady and her husband look mighty pleased with their heist, me being the bounty. The husband is driving, and the lady is trying to pet me, saying things like, home, love, my baby, warm, play, toys, bed, and what not. I am anxious and confused, due to which my listening abilities have diminished, and all I do is stare at her with a blank look in my eyes. I am rendered catatonic.

I thought you were my friend, lady! Why would you do this to me? All the nice things I said about you, I take it back. All the happy thoughts I thought about you, I take those back too. Your deceitful enterprise is now unravelled. Dye has been cast.

The moving finger has writ. Stop patronizing me! I will feign the inability to acknowledge your words.

I am trying to be aloof, and that will remain my modus operandi until I regain my powers to deduce and understand the hell that is happening. Do what you want, say what you want lady, but now, Mithi will no longer be sweet for you.

My trust issues now,

Are as deep as the sea,

I've built walls and

Locked my heart,

No one will find the key.

Chapter 6

GIVE A DOG A HOME

I think of you as God's gift, since I found you without looking, and ended up loving you, without trying.

Forms are filled and submitted, house check is complete and deemed positive, and by late evening, all formalities are finally complete. We inform our parents about our impromptu plans to adopt little Mithi, and are encouraged by them for the same. Our families share our excitement and happiness. We are thrilled. We are ready to adopt! Ready to bring home the little rescued dancing dog. Ready to love her, and share our heart and home with her.

Emotions run wild. In anticipation to adopt, and to experience our first taste of parenthood, we drive to the market on the way, and pick up a few pet essentials like leash, collar, toys, bowls, treats, woolen jacket etc. and head over to the farm for Mithi.

The caretakers at the farm are waiting for us, expecting us. We go in as quietly as we can, and get Mithi out without disrupting the peace and sleep time of the other dogs. Remember I told you about the 'I bark, you bark, we all bark' syndrome, and its acoustics effects. Yes, we did not want to trigger that scene.

Mithi is overjoyed to see us again. She also commences to perform her 'happy dance' routine for us once again, before we quickly whisk her away towards the exit, where our car is parked. She looks around, confused and baffled. Her happiness devolves into stress. We know what she must be going through, and we understand her befuddled mind frame. A situation like this is bound to bring anxiety and doubt in her mind, especially considering her past, where she was abused and abandoned and what not. All her former buried nightmares would certainly come revisiting her in a scenario like this.

Mandeep lifts her gently, and puts her in the backseat of our car. She is taken off guard and does not look pleased. With a whimper here, and a whine there, she is making vehement efforts to make her displeasure known, and is absolutely not willing to be a silent spectator. We bid adieu to the team at the farm, and with the whiny dog at the back seat, head back home.

I try to stroke her, whispering sweet nothings to her, in an attempt to soothe her frayed nerves. She is determinedly aloof and detached, unlike her previous self. Her eyes reflect feelings of confusion and betrayal. She is probably trying hard to gauge the current situation and absorb the enormity of it all.

We would have to remain patient, and build her trust in us, from scratch. We would have to keep trying to make her as comfortable as possible, until she knows, we are her family now. It will not happen in one day, or anytime soon, we were aware of that fact. We were ready to take the plunge nonetheless.

To bring this little doggo home, to give her the love, warmth, food, shelter, safety, that she was craving for, and probably never had experienced before, we were looking forward to it.

Our trip back home was the beginning of a new journey in our life.

Chapter 7

THE LAIR

Difficult roads often lead to beautiful destinations.

Looks like we have reached the den, their lair. I wonder what happens next! What is it they want from me? My guess is as good, or as bad, or as ugly, as yours.

Ransom? But who would give them a ransom for me?

My treats? But I ate them all.

My fur? My organs? But I am doggo, they are humans, it won't work, will it.

Whatever it is they expect, I shall not give it to them that easily. I would fight back like a ninja and escape from their evil clutches. I'll be slick. I'll be vigilant and watchful. I am treading on eggshells here. I resolve to remain alert henceforth. I will have to keep my eyes and ears open, at all times. I will also have to keep my sniffer activated, at all times.

The lady and the driver are now escorting me out of the car, and taking me to a room. It's a small room. The door is shutting now. Woahhhh! What is happening? What in tarnation is this sorcery? The room is moving. *OMG! Help! Someone? Anyone? Save the little doggo first!* This strange room car is moving upwards.

With no help in sight, apart from the lady and the driver, who are looking at me and smiling, I decide to help myself. I hold on tight, bend my legs, and grip my paws to the floor. I am crouching, like a mighty beast. It seems to work, the 'room car' stops. *Phew!* Be still my heart, you survived the ordeal. The door to the 'room car' opens, we walk out, and now they are taking me into a house.

Welcome home, the lady says to me, and kisses me on my head. I am not flattered, neither am I impressed. I burnt my paws before, so hell no, not again lady, you cannot dupe me again with love. Once bitten twice shy. You fool me once, shame on you, fool me twice shame on me. *Talk to the paw!*

Hmm. The house is warm. It smells nice too. Now what?

The lady pours water in a new bowl, and offers the same to me. I lap it up. I'm thirsty. I am also tired and equally stressed. Her husband, the driver, offers me treats. I gobble them up. Fun fact - stress eating is not a myth people!

Out of nowhere, the lady produces a wet towel, and starts cleaning me up. Ugh! What an inconvenience. I feel violated. To make matters worse, I am hugged and kissed too, by her. *Stinking pedophile!* Finally, I am let loose to explore the house. I wander in all the rooms, making notes, taking it all in.

Dinner is being prepared. The lady is cooking and I am relishing the aromas tickling my sniffer. Wonder if I'll get to taste what's cooking. Her husband probably hears my thoughts, and quickly offers me more treats. At least he is not stingy with treats, like his wackadoodle wife. I accept the treats uncomplainingly, because I am always hungry. But be warned, one and all, my love does not have a price. You may bribe me with food and treats to enter your room, sit on comfortable rugs, lie down, close my eyes, get some sleep; BUT you cannot buy my love with food and treats.

So now that I am in a slightly comfortable position, curled up on a warm rug, my tummy full and my eyes drooping with sleep; my stress levels have diminished considerably. I will shut my snout and my eyes, and try to catch up on my sleep. Tomorrow is another day. I will conquer tomorrow. My battle will be fought valiantly by me, and I will zzzzzzzzzzz

Chapter 8

THE HOME COMING

Home is where love resides,

Where memories are created,

And laughter never ceases,

Home is a family's pride.

Out of the frying pan into the fire, was the factual – 'out of the car into the elevator' proverbial tryst for Mithi. She was stumped and completely mystified in the moving elevator.

Once back home, we welcome Mithi in with open arms, into our warm abode. I wish I could tell her how I felt about her. How I already thought of her as part of my family. How she had nothing to fear and feel distressed about. How her life would only get better hereon. I feel immensely protective towards her. The connection that I felt when I saw her in the morning somehow grew stronger and I could very well understand the predicament of this little dog in my home, following me, with her tiny paws.

Offering her water and treats to make her comfortable, we decide to let her be, to explore, to sniff, and to get familiar with her new surroundings. She needs space, she needs time and she also needs a little sprucing up. I quickly sponge her with a towel to get rid of all the dirt and dust she is covered in. For now, this would do, however tomorrow, she would need intensive cleaning and washing, I think to myself.

We try and make her feel at home and give her a few toys we got for her. She shows no interest in the array of toys displayed before her, and is still aloof and standoffish, but she keeps her eyes on me, and continues to shadow me.

While I am preparing dinner, Mandeep is keeping her occupied with treats and toys. She sits where she can see me cooking in the kitchen. Mandeep and I decide to visit a veterinary tomorrow for her, and get her complete tests and checkup done, along with few basic, necessary grooming procedures. I make a mental note of all the queries I have for the veterinary, regarding her skin infection and persisting cough.

After dinner, we take her to the bedroom with us, where we make her lay on a comfortable rug. She looks exhausted, as are we. Stroking her head, I wish her a good night's sleep. She looks warm and cozy, curled up like a little ball of wool. In no time, she is fast asleep. I hope and pray that her nightmares don't trouble her tonight.

Sleep tight little one,

For your new life has already begun!

Chapter 9

NIGHT FRIGHT

Ghosts of the past, recast;

Dodging them, trying to escape,

I run far, I run fast.

I wake up with a start. It was a bad dream that woke me from my deep slumber. I shake myself off and rid myself of any nightmare residue left within. I don't want any scary thoughts lingering on me and my fur body.

Wait! Where am I again? I feel like that chick, Alice, lost in wonderland, left wandering and wondering. I blink in the darkness, trying to see and find my bearings. Takes me a while to realize I'm no longer in the farm. I'm in the house, in the room, with those two humans. That lady and her husband. I can see them sleeping peacefully on the bed. They look comfortable. *Not for long humans. Wait and watch! Karma is a lady dog! And that is me. I am karma for you. I will bite you on your voluptuous behind without any guilt.*

It's pretty quiet and peaceful in here. Maybe a little too quiet for my liking. *Hehe!* I will soon start to make some noise and create a ruckus. All my dramatic moves and tactics will come into play tonight. This is the perfect opportunity for me to show them what they got themselves into. I will make them realize, apologize, and regret their decision to dognap me. *You messed with the wrong doggo guys.* I will make this night an eventful one for you both; one that you'll remember with distaste for the rest of your life.

Mission – 'Karma is a lady dog'- activated. I shall now make my presence felt.

I start with my notorious whining and whimpering. Hmmmm… No reaction from these two sleepy heads. I do a louder version of the same. Ok, some movement. I decide to go nearer to the lady, and target her. I see her face. She looks innocent, unlike her evil self that I was subjected to, when she was awake. Let me share some facts, or gyan, as some of you may call it. Tried and tested facts. Lesson for all to learn.

First – Looks are deceptive. Do not judge a person looking innocent as being innocent. That person may be wicked and evil. Case in point, the lady in front of my eyes.

And second, loud moaning and groaning sounds, if exclaimed near a human's face, accompanied along with a few retching noises in between, is a sure shot deal to make the human sit erect, from whatever deep stages of sleep he/she maybe in. Case in point, me, doing the moaning, groaning and retching.

Both of them are wide awake and the lady is fussing over me. I continue my uproar. Mission in progress, I demand immediate attention and create a little chaos. I have gained remarkable fluency in theatrics. The lady is now up and about, wearing her shoes, covering her head with a funny looking woolen cap, wrapping herself in a warm coat, and telling her husband she is taking me down.

Excuse me lady, if you don't mind, I would like you to end the banal chit chat and feel the full extent of my wrath. Down? What is down? What did I get myself into now? *Lady! Where is down? Do we have food there?*

I am leashed and taken out of the house, where the lady presses a button, and lo and behold, the 'room car' door opens. We enter, I crouch, we travel, I survive yet again, door opens, we exit and we reach down.

Down is where we go to relieve ourselves. It is a cold winter night. *Dark, lonely and eerie.* Perfect for some exploring and sniffing escapades. I feel fresh like a daisy after my nap, but the lady looks like crap. She is half asleep, strolling around with me on a leash, watching me pee. *Creep alert!*

Down is nice. I want to spend some more time there but the lady is a buzzkill. She takes me back to the house and in the room, tucks me back in, on my rug bed, removes her shoes, cap, and all the paraphernalia, and goes back to bed. She thinks she can sleep peacefully? Sly lol!! No Ma'am, you can most definitely forget about it. Doggo mission is in progress, I will strike again. And again. And yet, again.

I am happy to report that my mission is successful, and the lady did not get a wink of sleep tonight. I did not let her sleep ☺ I managed to make her take me 'down' two more times just for fun, making her think that I had to pee or/and poo. Now she and I are sitting in the balcony of the house, star gazing. I am not letting her out of sight, prohibiting her to go inside and get in the bed.

As long as we both are sitting out in the balcony, amidst these strange looking pots and plants, inhaling the fresh air, feeling the icy cold breeze to the bone, listening to the lady's chattering teeth while she shivers, I am being reasonably quiet. But going inside is not an option for her.

Checkmate! Doggo wins this round, lady. Karma has struck and is dancing victoriously to the tunes of your chattering teeth. Must be humbling to bow down in defeat to this mighty doggo!

It was a fun night for me, can't say the same about the lady though. Although, I would like to acknowledge the fact that she thankfully, did not leave me alone in the balcony, and stayed with me, covering me with a warm blanket. I liked that. I got some treats too. I certainly liked that too.

Being the hallmark of a good doggo, and being a stickler for the doggo social convention decree - of always displaying happiness and gratefulness, I thanked the lady with few kisses and affection. It's almost morning now, and I can't wait to see what lies in store for me today.

Chapter 10

SLEEP WALKING

When life gives you lemons; return the lemons; and ask for coffee!!

I make yet another cup of coffee for myself before I head back to the cold embrace of the icy winds waiting for me in my balcony. Sun is not out yet, but the morning birds have started tweeting their happy tunes.

My whiny stalker, as usual, follows me around, from the balcony, to the kitchen, tracking each and every move I make. I share a biscuit with her and stroke her head with love. She seems happy and grateful. Wagging her little tail, she accepts my love and the biscuit with pleasure.

Coffee is keeping me awake and also keeping me going. I have been up and about since midnight, woken up by Mithi's cries and whimpers. Nothing seemed to comfort her. Maybe she felt confined and suffocated in the room, that's why she wouldn't stop crying. Or maybe she needed to relieve herself, or she just wanted to be outdoors for a bit.

Whatever the case maybe, I thought I'll take her downstairs for a stroll. So, we went down at midnight, and indeed, she did stop crying. I think she felt much better after the midnight stroll, where I practically sleep walked. As long as we were downstairs, she seemed happy, but the moment I brought her back home, she again started crying.

She wanted to go down again. It was like the lion had tasted blood. I tried my best to get her to bed, but this doggo would have none of it. Not wanting to disturb Mandeep, I got Mithi to the second bedroom, where I offered her our bed to sleep on, alongside me. She still continued her whining.

I finally had to take her downstairs again. Winter is at its peak, and it's terribly cold. But I had no choice. We repeated the whole go down, stroll, come back, whine again shebang two more times, after which, I decided enough is enough, and I took her to the balcony.

Thankfully, she was satisfied being there, as long as I was there too, braving the cold. Well, she is vulnerable and is still adjusting to her new environment. It is bound to take time and she is bound to feel confined and restrained in a new home, I remind myself.

So that was my first night with Mithi, 'my little stalker', as I had started to address her thus. Sleepless, yawn inducing, coffee guzzling, cold bearing, shivering through multiple layers of woolens and blankets wrapped around me, sitting on my chair in my balcony, looking fondly at the little doggo who is staring back at me. Do I see a glimmer of trust and love in her eyes??

Maybe the night, which taught me patience, taught her to trust.

As if on cue, she gets up, does the cutest downward dog stretch, and wagging her little tail, comes towards me, giving me soft kisses on my hand. My God, she is a sweetheart. I let her get close to me and gain confidence and trust in me. She is rubbing her body against my legs now decidedly wanting more pets and more scratches from me. Great! I oblige willingly.

After a while, I get up to go inside. She follows me as usual. I go to the second bedroom and get comfortable on the bed; she jumps up on the bed too, and sits in the far end corner. This time, she doesn't whimper and she doesn't whine. I am glad. *Let's sleep for a while sweety*, I tell her. She doesn't complain. She lays down, her eyes still on me, following my each and every move. I smile to myself. I know what I'm going to name her!

Chapter 11

MY RECHRISTENING

Breaking News!

I have had an epiphany. I feel enlightened. And slightly embarrassed and foolish too, if I may add.

You see, I was under the impression that I have been taken hostage by these two humans, and my torturous days are back. But I am happy to reveal that all my fears and doubts have vanished now. These two have seemingly no evil intentions towards me and my existence. They are in fact pampering me, and showering lots of love on me. I may have been quick to judge and I misjudged them. But, they are nice and I am beginning to open my heart to them.

And oh, by the way, I have been gifted a new name, which I will now be responding to. Without further ado, lo and behold world, I now present my lovely self to you, as 'Shadow'.

So, despite my last night's theatrics, the lady had been totally indulging me with patience and affection. She did not lose her temper even once. After spending last night together, gallivanting down and then in the balcony, I finally allowed the lady to get some sleep. We came inside at the crack of dawn, and slept peacefully for an hour or so this morning in the other bedroom. I did not disturb the lady this time even though I kept my surveillance on her while she slept. But I did not wake her up and I let her continue to sleep.

The husband arose and sauntered in from the other room. He looked well rested. He was glad to see me snoozing with the lady. He stroked my head with love before asking me to come with him. I wasn't sure, until I saw the biscuit and my leash in his hand. Was he taking me 'down'? Ok I'm game. Let's go driver.

Yes, we went down. He took me for a long walk and I was overjoyed. I got the opportunity to explore the vast area and my sniffer had a thorough workout. I met many humans and dogs too. I liked most of them, most of them liked me too, and the rest were very barkable.

After our walk, coming back to the house, I ran inside to tell the lady about my walk experience. She was still asleep and this time I woke her up with my licker, my way of giving kisses.

Finally, the lady roused and she is now making breakfast for us. *Yayy!* (happy dance). BUT, I am expected to wait outside the kitchen. *How lame!* Kitchen is my favorite room in the house. It has food in there. I love food. And food aroma emerging from the kitchen is my definition of heaven air. However, apparently, I am banned from going inside the kitchen. I'm exiled out of the kitchen. I am prohibited from entering the most interesting area of the house. *Why lady? Why on earth you do such things??* As though, I will ruin the sanctity of the blessed food place. So unfair! *Lady! You better check yourself, before you wreck yourself.*

You can keep the food away from Shadow, but you cannot keep Shadow away from food. You will be deemed constitutionally incapable of trying to meddle with the doggo - kitchen relationship paradigm. I will find a way to unban myself. All that food will be mine.

Well, the only thing better than talking and thinking about food, is eating food. My food is here, in my doggie bowl. Table manners dictate not talking while chomping on food. So I'll catch you all later. Bon Appetite!

Chapter 12

SHADOW IT IS

Happiness starts with a wet nose, and ends with a wagging tail.

I woke up to gentle kisses and sniffs. Feeling the cold wet nose booping me on my face was enough to wake me up with a smile. So henceforth, my alarm clock is going to be cold and wet I gather.

Mandeep was already awake and had been considerate enough to not wake me before. He knew I had a long night. He said he had taken Mithi for a walk already. *Shadow*, I said. Shadow? He asked. Yes! Shadow. Because she has been shadowing me ever since she saw me. She is my Shadow.

What a perfect name for this little stalker.

So our morning started with a sumptuous breakfast. Shadow too, enjoyed her meal, and after polishing off the last tiny bit of morsel in her bowl, came running excitedly to me, kissing and licking my hand. How adorable!!

I wish more humans could have the 'Attitude of gratitude' personality, as exuded by animals. We have so much to learn from them. Ironically, they have more humanity in them than us humans could ever have. If only we could learn.

Right now, I am doing the laundry, with Shadow besides me, looking absolutely baffled at the washing machine and the washing noise coming from therein. Her little head tilts, while trying to gauge the washing machine, are hilarious.

She is wonderstruck. Can't wait to see her reaction to the noise of the mixer grinder and the hoover.

Mandeep has already left for work and I am trying to finish doing the household chores with Shadow doing what she does best, following me. She is settling in well, and I intend to spend quality one – on – one time with her to make her transition from Shelter to our home easier.

Thankfully, I work as a freelancer and can opt to take a sabbatical from work as and when required. In fact, I had always been working in a fast paced, corporate environment, and now since the last three years, I had decided to slow down and take a breather. Hence, the freelancing, which gave me ample opportunity to devote my free time doing things that truly made me happy, and spending time with people who really mattered to me. I felt no embarrassment in accepting the fact that I was no longer the professionally ambitious person that I was, a few years back. Now I'm happily free spirited and footloose. And I decide to do full justice to the commitment we made when we adopted Shadow by giving her my time, and training her with patience.

By mid-day, we start getting visitors. My friends and few children from our society, wanting to meet the latest addition in our family, drop in to welcome Shadow in our midst. Shadow is overwhelmed. She happily greets everyone, and does her little happy dance each time someone visits. All are privy to her dancing chops now. This girl has some serious dance moves which come so naturally to her, each time there is a burst of happiness in her heart. I can watch that butt wiggle and that belly jiggle all day long!

I remind myself about the veterinary appointment in the evening for Shadow's checkup, vaccination and of course grooming. Did I mention she is a little stink bomb. Yes, I did clean her up yesterday night, but she needed intensive grooming, which the vet said she would administer. Yeah! All those kisses and rubs Shadow gave me today, were infused with her stinky aroma, but I did not complain. It wasn't too bad, really!

So once Mandeep returned home, we headed to the vet with Shadow. And this time there was comparatively lesser whining coming through the backseat of the car from her. Well, that's a start for sure. ☺

Chapter 13

BE PAWSITIVE

If you're happy and you know it, do the dance!!!

I am the new kid on the block. The good-looking, mysterious, enigmatic stranger you all read about in novels. That's me! Word spread about my smoldering good looks and tremendous adorability like wildfire I guess. So lots of people came to see me today. I welcomed them all. But their arrival was preceded by a very strange, loud, ear wrecking noise. I am no stranger to noise, but I have to admit, humans have quirky bizarre appliances in their homes which yield even more bizarre noises. Each time the strange noise was made, I barked my head off with confusion, after which the lady opened the main door, and the guests came in. That was our sequence of events.

The lady introduced me happily to everyone and I was just as charming as ever. The spotlight shone on me all day. I was the superstar. Everyone adored me and my happy dance. I felt so loved and so popular. I'm so glad to be here. The lady is nice too, but she just moves around too much. It gets difficult to keep tabs on her movements, especially with so many guests around, vying for my attention.

Later during the day, we went down for a walk in the park

again. It was awesome. Us walking together feels like beauty walking the beast (me being the beauty of course). Then once back in the house, I parked myself in a strategic position where the lady remained in my peripheral vision zone. I tried having my afternoon siesta there, though it was constantly interrupted by the lady not being stationary. She can't be doing random this and that, while I try and get my forty winks. I will need to train her. Soon!

Woof woof bark bark... Lady!! Help!!! It's that loud irksome noise again. My little flapping ears feel so hackneyed.

On my cue, she goes and opens the door. *Oh my gawd! Yayyy! He is back…* The driver had left the house in the morning after breakfast, with a big bag which did not smell of food, and a small bag, which had a box, that smelt of delicious food. He said bye to the lady, and to me before leaving, and I was sad to see him go, thinking I would not see him again. But look, here he is. With those bags. I am greeting him in, welcoming him, with my dance. *Lady! Join me. Let us all dance. And let us all eat.*

Well!

We are in the car, again. The driver is driving, the lady is being annoying, and I'm clueless, again. I don't know where they are taking me, again. *Déjà vu!!* Just when everything is going good, and we are all getting along fine, why ruffle my feathers, rather fur? I whine a little to show my displeasure.

Lady I want to go back to the house. Doctor? What? Stinky? Dirty? Me?? Bath?? No no no... Excuse me lady!! What are you talking about? Maybe you have the wrong doggo. I need no doc, no bath, no grooming. These plebeian tasks are not meant for me. Au contraire! I am fine. I am lovely. Ughh!! This lady is just so pedestrian! Someone take this lady away before I barrage her with my cacophonous assault of words.

'I smell as fresh as a rose,

But the lady thinks I'm supremely gross'.

Finally, the car stops. We are at the veterinary clinic. I am not happy. Oh my Dawg, what's going to happen now!

FYI, not so fun fact, rather a scathing indictment that ought to be noted by all:

The vets are friendly people until they start poking and pinching you here and there. They scan your body – *from ears to rears*, shamelessly with probing hands and then discuss about your body with others. *Pervert much!* I feel so objectified. And to top it all, they also make you ingest bitter stuff, puncture your skin with needles and the worst of all, insert a strange looking object into your bum, and then read what your bum wrote on it. *Yikes!*

If this is not enough, they also groom you. Yes, you heard it right! They trim your claws, brush your teeth, put you in a scary looking tub and clean you like a ragged washcloth. *The horror! The torture!*

If sham*poo* has *poo* in it, why slather and lather it on? Let's just roll in poo like we are supposed to. But no, you got to wash, lather, rinse and repeat for some reason. I had to go through all the above mentioned atrocities because, get this, the lady thought 'I needed it'. *Yeah right!*

I need you to mind your own business lady!! And don't even for a second forget that I missed to notice your utterly failed attempts of trying to conceal your giggles watching me bathe.

This little black dog has saved this offending data in her little black box and is bound to retrieve it, analyze it, and use it for future quality and training purpose. Mind it!!

Finally, after I have been washed, cleaned, dried, and have been announced as 'squeaky clean', we are heading back to the house I presume. Unless they are taking me to the 'cleanest doggo' contest, which I am sure I'll nail. I have had a really wet and frothy evening and I'm (sham)pooped out now.

Chapter 14

(WET)ERINARY VISIT

*"I'm not laughing at you; I'm laughing with you" said all those
who laughed at you.*

At the clinic, Shadow is met with a lot of enthusiasm by her
vet and the staff. They are happy to see the little rescued
dancing dog, coping well after adoption. Shadow too meets
them happily and is taken in by the treats and praises. All is
hunky dory for Shadow, until the professionals get down to
business. Then she tenses.

Her file is made, and she is then put on the sterilized table.
She cowers and looks frightened. She is trembling. We are
right there besides her to comfort her. She looks at me for
assurance and I assure her everything will be fine, and we'll
be back home soon.

She is given a thorough check by her vet. Her temperature is
normal, but her skin allergy and kennel cough are a cause of
concern. Also, her mammary glands are swollen. We would
need to get her sterilized in the future. She is administered the
necessary vaccines that were due. Her deworming needs to be
done as well. The vet prescribes medicines and supplements
for her, explaining to me the dosage and frequency of each,
and I diligently take notes. After Shadow's vaccinations and

deworming papers are made, and are brought up to date, she is released from the table.

She heaves a sigh of relief and shakes herself of all anxiety. Too soon Missy! I think to myself. She pulls us towards the exit with her leash, in a hurry to exit the clinic. Hang on!! You have a grooming session to go to now, I tell her.

The assigned staff takes us to a room that contains a huge metal tub for animal bathing. Ok! Fun times ahead, Mandeep and I look at each other knowingly. This will be worth recording, but we decide against it. We know Shadow would not go in easily, and even if she does, she won't stay in quietly. Shadow probably senses what is in store for her and starts bolting. The staff, experienced and accustomed, lifts her and enters the bath tub with her, to her surprise. She is aghast, and looks at all our faces with incredulity. Her skepticism is palpable.

Ok, I am not proud of what I did in there, and I am sorry I did it, but I could not help myself. I giggled at Shadow.

And I am absolutely ashamed to admit, that I laughed out loud as well, at Shadow.

And I am even sorrier to tell you that if Mandeep had not stopped me, I would have been literally rolling on the floor laughing my guts out, at Shadow.

This dog is so dramatic!!

From the martyred look on her face; to the conniving look - presumably planning our assassination.

From the 'I will escape this torture and not suffer in silence' look, to the 'a little to the right, yes here, that's the spot, I am enjoying the scrub, thank you Sir' look.

It was hilarious. Her expressions were laughably transparent and I was out of control. Well to be fair to me, I really could not help it. Many a times in life, I have faced the embarrassment of uncontrollable giggles emerging from my mouth, (especially in situations where complete silence is solicited), while my brain is screaming at me to shut up.

It has happened in school when our class was being reprimanded, in college when I saw a professor fall, in my workplace - during a meeting, and so on….

The list is truly, very long. Basically these 'giggling attacks' have diverse triggers. And these attacks, once triggered, cannot be repressed, suppressed or any other pressed. Call it a manufacturing defect or a forever rising embarrassment fountain. But watching Shadow being bathed and then dried and groomed, I learned two things, firstly, she looks like a wet rat and hates baths, and secondly, my giggles cannot be tamed.

So, I might as well have a laugh now, before I go back home to another long, sleepless night with Shadow during her acclimatization phase.

Chapter 15

HOME IS A FEELING

All hail this blessed place that beholds before my squinty eyes. I now pronounce thee, my home!!

It feels so good to be back. I am beginning to love this familiar, comforting and warm place. This is my home now. My abode. And I proclaim today, that I am never leaving this home again, except for when I go down, to pee and poo.

Coming back home, felt so surreal. So comforting. Like for us dogs, finding the right spot to poop after holding it in for hours. Or for you humans, like removing shoes, after a long day at work, shoes that were a size smaller to your feet. Get it? Or for better effect, imagine those tight shoes, being worn all day, in the wrong feet. Now get it?? And the sweet release, once you take off those shoes. SIGH OF RELIEF!! Yes, that's exactly the same feeling I was experiencing now. This is my homecoming.

Home is where the lady is. Home is where her husband is. Home is where my bed is. Home is where my food and water bowls are. And most important, home is where the kitchen with food is. My belly roars as I see the lady in the kitchen, getting my bowl of food ready for me. *High time lady! Stop slacking and start packing.* Hurry up, will you. This super clean, fragrance radiating, shine illuminating doggo is famished. *Chop Chop!!*

So… We are all lounging in the living room, watching a big box stuck on the wall. It is noisy. It has surround sound, light and images on it. Magical? No, witchcraft I say! Why are we looking at that box? Beats me. Humans are weird. Maybe the poor box is crying and complaining since it's stuck on the wall. Whatever! I have problems of my own to ruminate on.

You know, even though I ate my meal a while back, I am still a tad curious to see what the lady and her husband are snacking on. They kept the good snacks for themselves it seems. And they are not sharing. Must train them to share.

Hmm…I have come to the conclusion, that it's not just me, even these two humans living here, are big time food lovers. They apparently had snacks, and then they had dinner too. And did they share with the doggo? No Sir, they did not. *Gluttons!*

And the lady kept saying 'No' to me when I came closer to their food; or even looked at their food. Mean, right? She sure is bossy. Her husband is nicer. He tried to give me tit bits, but she stopped him and said some crazy jibber jabber stuff like 'She'll get spoilt, learn bad habits, will beg for food, training has started, bla bla bla'. I did not get any tit bits. Miss bossy pants wouldn't let me.

Hey lady! You are not the boss of me. I am my own boss, my own CEO, my own manager. You don't own me. Do you copy? I told her. Telepathically. She ought to learn soon. One cannot tame the wild. I'm savage. I'm a beast. You just don't go around saying 'No' to a wild beast! The beast will not like that, at all. Oh hey, I got to go; the lady is calling me.

My colloquial 'after dinner, before sleep' walk with the lady and her husband was a good finale to the day. I am really sleepy now, and I am all curled up in my bed. I know I will not be asleep for long. Maybe the events of last night will be revisited, or maybe not. Who knows? I'm an enigma, a force to reckon with. My mysteriousness is sometimes a mystery to me as well. My heart, mind and body, is the epitome of the famous Bermuda triangle. Who knows what I'll think, feel or do? 'Enchanting mystery', thy name is Shadow.

The lady is still in my periphery vision and my eyes are still very much on her, until my blinks get drowsy, and she gets blurry, more blurrr zzzzzzzz…

Chapter 16

LOVE IS A FOUR-LEGGED WORD

'Heavens go by favor. If it went by merit, you would stay out and your dog would go in' – Mark Twain.

Shadow has been with us for fifteen days now, and after her initial 'acclimatization phase' (sleepless nights for me) which lasted about four days / nights, she has settled in nicely.

My days are spent primarily training her, making her learn and obey commands, feeding her, walking her, playing with her, spending time with her, understanding her personality and nursing her back to health. There is a stark change in her, for the better; physically, mentally and emotionally.

Shadow, in return, loves Mandeep and me wholeheartedly. She is extremely affectionate, responsive and obedient. A truly well behaved and playful little dog, she is an absolute delight. We have discovered our own unspoken language. She understands our moods, our tone of voice and even our facial expressions and eye indications. That's how strong our connection has become. She is absolutely devoted to us. And yes, she still shadows me around, always keeping an eye on me.

It's true; every dog is a product of its environment. A dog, when treated right and handled with love; will turn out to be the perfect companion.

Jodi Preis quoted,

"Every dog starts life with a blank canvas. His destiny etched by the hands of the painter, and each one an artist's original. The portrait painted depends on how the brush is held.

Paint with hostility, and a dog learns to fight.

Paint with cruelty, and a dog learns to fear.

Paint with anger, and a dog learns aggression.

Paint with praise, and a dog learns confidence.

Paint with boundaries, and a dog learns respect.

Paint with tenderness, and a dog learns to bond.

Paint with affection, and a dog learns to love.

Every dog is a product of its environment. Bad dogs are not born, they are created. If the portrait is flawed, look to the artist. Stop blaming the dogs!"

Dogs in fact, can teach you more lessons about the art of living life, than any life coach or any self-help book ever could. To be a better person, and to live life to the fullest, just follow the below mentioned dog rules, and learn these basic fundamentals from the Dog.

Dog Wisdom – from the Dog!

* Love unconditionally and love without expectations.

* Be loyal, faithful and dependable.

* Be content and show gratitude, always.

* When you see your loved ones, run to greet them with enthusiasm.

* Seize every moment and live in that moment.

* Be brave, no matter what size you are.

* Sniff out opportunities and take chances.

* Take frequent naps.

* Accept yourself. Be silly. Don't be embarrassed. Like, if you fall down; get back up, shake it off, forget about it, and go on.

* Delight in the simple joys of a long walk.

* Make new friends.

* Learn new tricks, no matter your age.

* Play every day. Never stop playing.

* Have fun, lots of it. Make your own fun.

* Jump with joy when happy.

* Play hard, sleep harder.

* Drink lots of water.

* Don't hold grudges. Forgive quickly.

* Wag more, bark less.

* Sometimes, it is alright to just eat and sleep the whole day.

* Ride through life with the window open. Enjoy your journey.

* Appreciate every bite of what you eat.

* Accept gratefully what is being offered to you.

* Chase your dreams.

* Protect those you love.

* Show passion and love with gusto.

* Have no regrets.

* At the end of the day, always snuggle with loved ones, no matter how the day was.

If only we could imbibe these guidelines like the dogs, the world would become a much better place to live in!

Well, Mandeep and I have a road trip planned in a few days, and I sure hope Shadow remembers to imbibe these dog rules then. Fingers crossed! Let's hope that her tail wagging, pure adoration and unrestrained affection, continues and remains intact throughout. Amen!

Chapter 17

PAWS AND ENJOY THE GOOD LIFE

Finally! I have a place to call home, and a family to call my own.

I am living life, queen size. I have my own personal butler, driver, trainer, walker, nutritionist, cook, playmates, parents and caregiver in these two humans, I now call my family.

I address them as Mandeep and Nisha, because duh! you know, that is, their name. While they call me names like, Shadow, Shadowvey, chota Shadow, baby, bagheera, bhaalu, golu, motu etc.. I respond to all names directed towards me. I am the doggo with multiple aliases and pseudonyms. Life is good. I am living the suite and sweet life.

I feel like a comet. Why comet? Because a comet is a star that has a tail, and I have a tail too. I'm a star with a tail.

Having somewhere to go, is a home, and having someone to love, is family.

My family, unbeknownst to my knowledge, fell in love with me at first sight. They picked me from amongst the throng, got me home and placed me in their hearts. They did not care about the way I looked or that I wasn't a pedigree. They loved me for being me.

They showed me that I'm not disposable and that I am capable of being loved and cherished. They have gone out of their way to bring back the sparkle in my eyes and the shine on my coat. They have restored my spirit, my health, and my faith. This little ray of sunshine that is me, is ready to beam again and dazzle one and all. ☺

I did not think it possible, but you'll be surprised to know that now my tail wags even more, all because of them. And I continue to Rock n Roll doing my happy dance. At the risk of sounding redundant, I love my life and I love my family.

It has been fifteen days now, and counting. A roller coaster ride full of new experiences, new adventures and a whole new life. Initially I was extremely skeptical about everything, since all this was absolutely alien to me. My fragile ecosystem was shaken up and heavily impacted by the tsunami of new elements like home, family, loving hands, bowl of food and water, bed, sweet nothings, playtime and so on, and so forth, and what have you. But I have adapted, and how!

I have adjusted Mandeep and Nisha with myself, and they are as much a part of me, as I am, a part of them.

Improving on perfection is a highly challenging task, and I must applaud Nisha for her efforts to improve my being. She has taken it upon herself to train me.

I know you all must be seriously shocked hearing this. I get it, I feel you. I was equally shocked and stunned when I realized what she was up to. This lady and her antics I tell you. I can barely spell etiquettes, and here, this woman wants me to be all well-mannered and obedient. *What a laugh!!* Do you know what is interesting about being trained? *Nothing! Literally nothing!*

But then again, you know I love treats right. Apparently, Nisha knows that too. And she holds the treats hostage until I follow some random commands like,

Sit,

Shake hands,

Other paw,

Give me high five,

Hands up,

Lay down,

Get up,

No,

Come here,

Let's go,

Stop chewing that,

Oh my God, what is in your mouth, do not swallow it…Etc etc….

I have learnt, and am still learning, quite a few tricks though. And I've been complimented on my obedience too. So maybe, I am crossing the plateau of perfection perfectly. And maybe, just maybe, a new benchmark for perfection could be created by yours truly Shadow, moi.

Ok Lady!! You train me and I train you,

And if it doesn't work, I blame you!! ☺

Chapter 18

TRIPLING

It does not matter where you are headed, or where you go; what matters is who you go with, and who you have besides you.

I have my husband and my Shadow besides me. Our road trip was a success and it was the first amongst many to follow. After the initial hiccups, Shadow has become a pro traveller and accompanies us to all of our adventurous holidays, trips and getaways. We, as a trio, have scoured through many destinations together. Experiences make memories, and we have lots of them, mostly fond ones.

Not just a travel partner, Shadow is our unswerving comrade, till date shadowing us, through all good and bad, happy and sad, high and low, exciting or dull moments.

Love is not a sprint, it's a marathon.

It has been almost four years since we got the little black dancing dog home, and yet she continues to dance and love us each day, even more than the previous day. Is it even possible to love someone to that extent? I see the look in Shadow's eyes, and I know it is. My sunshine doesn't come from the skies; it comes from the love in my Shadow's eyes. She brings me sunshine and funshine! And furshine too.

In the past four years, dog hair has become a part of our home décor. It's everywhere. 'Fur'niture is called *fur*niture, for a reason. Cleaning a house that has a shedding dog, is equivalent to brushing your teeth while eating a kit-kat chocolate. You have got to cease your fruitless efforts to get rid of it, rather embrace the dog hair, and enjoy eating that frigging kit-kat chocolate (brush your teeth later).

Loyalty and love is worth every dog hair in your home. Our clothes and furniture might be covered in dog hair, but well, we love it. Who needs con-fetti, when you have fur-fetti.

Shadow has somehow managed to train us to share tit bits of our food with her. So yes, she is a little spoilt and pampered, and we shall continue to spoil her forever. She also continues to be the most well behaved, obedient and smart doggo, enticing us all with her perfect high fives and hands up tricks, and I am so proud of her.

Dogs understand their humans and their language, however convoluted in nature. And the glimmer of registering the keywords and the head tilts that follow on hearing those words, are a treat to watch.

One is never lonely in the company of a dog. Even in their silence, they somehow manage to show you how you mean the world to them. Be it their tail thumping when you smile at them or even look at them, or the way they come and rest against your leg and sit close to you, watching over you. They make you feel so special.

Shadow is also my very own, exclusive, no fee, 24*7, state of the art equipped, tail wagging gym. Because of her, I am active and I get my daily dose of cardio while walking her.

Our walks are the highlight of her day, and seeing her excited, motivates me to not skip our routinely walks. She has helped me stay in shape and not be lazy. In fact if it were up to her, she would whole heartedly and suggestively volunteer to eat all my food as well, so I do not gain weight. *Oh so considerate!*

By virtue of her boundless love and undying affection, this little fur ball has become an integral part of us. The joy of being greeted by her while entering the house (duration of time away from home ranging 30 seconds or/ and above), is unparalleled. The hurt in her eyes when being kissed goodbye, and the happiness in her eyes when she sees us, is pure love.

Before Shadow, Mandeep and I were a couple, now we are a family!

Her eyes follow me,

where ever I be.

My Shadow, my stalker,

is as cute as can be.

A rescue, a roadie,

a survivor, she is.

Still fighting with demons of her past,

in nightmares.

In spite of her traumatic past,

she is the kindest and happiest soul.

Sloppy kisses, welcome dance, warm cuddles,

giving us her whole...

Four years back we got her home,

who adopted whom,

is yet unknown!!

Chapter 19

FUREVER YOURS

You feed me when I'm hungry,

You keep water in my dish,

You let me sleep on anything,

Or in any place I wish.

You sometimes let me lick your hands,

Or even lick your face,

Despite the fact I've licked myself,

In every private place.

You taught me how to come when called,

You taught me how to sit,

You always let me go outside,

So I can take a sh*t.

You'll always have my loyalty,

Up to the bitter end.

Coz after all, it's plain to see,

You are my best friend.

~Author unknown

~Lines borrowed by Shadow

Dedicated to my mom and dad! Yeah people, this is Shadow, sharing lines from what you people call the internet, because this is exactly what I feel for my pawrents.

The lady, my mom, is still kind of annoying, but she's my mom, and I love her to bits. The driver, my best friend, he's the coolest dad who protects me, plays with me and gives me treats liberally (unlike my stingy, weight watching, calorie counting, 'shadow is already overweight' harping, mom).

I have had the time of my life in the last few years with my family. Togetherness is what I seek, whether at home, or away from home - holidaying, seeking adventure or exploring new places. I'm the quintessential spoilt child, getting my way most of the times. I don't ask for much anyways. All I need is love, care, pets, belly rubs, long walks so I can poo and pee in public, play time, uninterrupted and DND labelled sleep time, undivided attention, and a little food (just kidding! I need lots of food). That's all!! It's the little things that make me happy and keep me going!

As the years go rolling by, my excited rolls and somersaults still continue, but I keep them in check because my bones hurt now. I sleep more often because I get tired soon, however I continue to do the happy dance nevertheless. I have grayed a bit and I rock the salt and pepper look on me. I'm your very own 'doggo shaped configuration of dualism balance' of Yin and Yang, black and white.

Even though I'm growing older, and a little heavier, (I like to think of myself as - not fat, just fluffy, but we don't need to quibble over terminology), I'll be my mom and dad's puppy furever.

I'm their baby and I know it,

And I'm not afraid to show it,

I will not grow up and blow it,

I'm the pupcake and the apple of their eye :)

So long folks!

Thank you for lending me your ears. You've been terrific and I had a ball sharing my journey with you all.

I hope when you do find a Mithi somewhere, you think of me, and show her some kindness. Every dog deserves a chance. There are lots of Mithi's out there, take one in, you'll have a Shadow for life too, I promise!

Dog bless you all!!

Chapter 20

EVERY DOG HAPPENS FOR A REASON

Dogs have mysterious ways of finding people who need them most, and filling voids in their hearts and lives, which those people never even knew existed.

No wonder dogs are termed as the best therapists. They know how to fix you, without even trying. A 'Man's best friend', they offer their lifelong loyalty and companionship for even the slightest bit of kindness and love showered on them.

They are happy in your happiness, and a constant in your solitude. They do not judge you, or care about your physical appearance or social status. They love you just the way you are and in fact, love you more than they love themselves. Their love is pure, unconditional, unadulterated and wholesome, and they will continue to love you till the last beat of their heart. That's the Dog's purpose for you! Their existence is so relevant, so riveting.

This book, is for all those kindred souls, who have had the honor of knowing the love of a dog.

And for rest of those who think – 'It's just a dog', here is something that truly resonates with me, and all those who think like me.

~ ~ ~

~Unknown Author~

From time to time, people tell me, "lighten up, it's just a dog", or "that's a lot of money for just a dog".

They don't understand the distance travelled, the time spent, or the costs involved for "just a dog".

Some of my proudest moments have come about with "just a dog".

Many hours have passed and my only company was "just a dog", but I did not once feel slighted.

Some of my saddest moments have been brought about by "just a dog", and in those days of darkness, the gentle touch of "just a dog" gave me comfort and reason to overcome the day.

If you too think it's "just a dog", then you probably understand phrases like "just a friend", "just a sunrise", or "just a promise".

"Just a dog" brings into my life the very essence of friendship, trust, and pure unbridled joy.

"Just a dog" brings out the compassion and patience that make me a better person.

Because of "just a dog", I will rise early, take long walks and look longingly to the future.

So for me and folks like me, it's not "just a dog" but an embodiment of all the hopes and dreams of the future, the fond memories of the past, and the pure joy of the moment.

"Just a dog" brings out what's good in me and diverts my thoughts away from myself and the worries of the day.

I hope that someday they can understand that it's not "just a dog", but the thing that gives me humanity and keeps me from being "just a man" or "just a woman".

So the next time you hear the phrase "just a dog", just smile, because they "just don't understand".

~ ~ ~

ABOUT THE AUTHOR

Artist, poet, philanthropist, writer, home maker, animal lover and now, a published author, Harnisha Singh, has added yet  another feather to her cap. Having accomplished twelve years of diverse work culture experience, ranging from - Airline industry, banking sector, corporate sector, diplomatic missions and school administration, she's now an entrepreneur, running her own business venture. *I'm still a work in progress*, she says!

She is living her happily ever after in Gurgaon, with her husband, and her little black dancing dog, who claims to be her pupcake. A free-spirited soul, she likes to stay footloose and explore the world and various beautiful facets of life.

When she's not writing, she loves to read, watch movies, go swimming, or just hang out with friends and family. According to her husband, she is blissfully delusional about her singing and dancing capabilities. Music, good food, red wine and dark chocolate (not necessarily in that order) are her weakness.

'When you dig another out of their troubles, you find a place to bury your own' is the motto she lives by. A volunteer worker with Robin Hood Army and an animal rescuer, *she is a happy concoction, of reality and fairy dust, sprinkling sanity to chaos, with kindness, faith and trust.*

Mandeep and Shadow

Nisha and Shadow

Shadow and Nisha

Shadow